WONDER BOOKS®

Football

A Level Two Reader

By Cynthia Klingel and Robert B. Noyed

Punt, pass, and kick. It is time to play football!

A football is a funny shape. It is brown and made of leather.

FIDELITY
HESS
BUD LIGHT
GIANTS

Football is played on a large field. Goal posts are on both ends of the field.

Players must wear special gear. They wear a helmet on their head. A mask on the helmet protects the player's face.

35
23
22

Players wear pads on their shoulders, knees, and hips. They wear shoes with spikes on the bottom.

In a game, each team has 11 players on the field. The team called offense has the ball and tries to score. A score is called a touchdown.

22

EXIT
34
FALCONS
34

The other team is the defense. They try to keep the offense from scoring. They block players who have the ball.

If the offense scores, then the defense gets the ball. Or, if the offense does not move the ball down the field far enough, the defense gets the ball.

Every player on the team
has a different job. They
practice the skills they
need to do their job.

Football can be a rough sport. It can also be very fun to watch or play.

Index

To Find Out More

Books

Christopher, Matt, and Bill Ogden. *The Dog That Stole Football Plays.* Boston: Little, Brown, 1980.

Gibbons, Gail. *My Football Book.* New York: HarperCollins Publishers, 2000.

Helmer, Diana Star, and Thomas S. Owens. *The History of Football.* New York: PowerKids Press, 2000.

Kessler, Leonard. *Kick, Pass, and Run.* New York: HarperCollins Children's Books, 1996.

Web Sites

Visit our homepage for lots of links about football:
http://www.childsworld.com/links.html

Note to Parents, Teachers, and Librarians:
We routinely verify our Web links to make sure they're safe, active sites—so encourage your readers to check them out!

Note to Parents and Educators

Welcome to Wonder Books®! These books provide text at three different levels for beginning readers to practice and strengthen their reading skills. Additionally, the use of nonfiction text provides readers the valuable opportunity to *read to learn*, not just to learn to read.

These leveled readers allow children to choose books at their level of reading confidence and performance. Nonfiction Level One books offer beginning readers simple language, word choice, and sentence structure as well as a word list. Nonfiction Level Two books feature slightly more difficult vocabulary, longer sentences, and longer total text. In the back of each Nonfiction Level Two book are an index and a list of books and Web sites for finding out more information. Nonfiction Level Three books continue to extend word choice and length of text. In the back of each Nonfiction Level Three book are a glossary, an index, and a list of books and Web sites for further research.

State and national standards in reading and language arts emphasize using nonfiction at all levels of reading development. Wonder Books® fill the historical void in nonfiction material for primary grade readers with the additional benefit of a leveled text.

About the Authors

Cynthia Klingel has worked as a high school English teacher and an elementary school teacher. She is currently the curriculum director for a Minnesota school district. Cynthia lives with her family in Mankato, Minnesota.

Robert B. Noyed started his career as a newspaper reporter. Since then, he has worked in school communications and public relations at the state and national level. Robert lives with his family in Brooklyn Center, Minnesota.

Readers should remember...
All sports carry a certain amount of risk. To reduce the risk of injury while playing football, play at your own level, wear all safety gear, and use care and common sense. The publisher and author take no responsibility or liability for injuries resulting from playing football.

Published by The Child's World®
P.O. Box 326
Chanhassen, MN 55317-0326
800-599-READ
www.childsworld.com

Photo Credits
© Ariel Skelley/CORBIS: 2
© Dennis MacDonald/PhotoEdit: 14, 17
© Jim Cummins/CORBIS: 9, 21
© Joe McBride/Tony Stone: cover
© John Gichigi/GettyImages: 13
© Kelly-Mooner Photography/CORBIS: 6
© Lawrence Manning/CORBIS: 18
© Paul J. Sutton/CORBIS: 5, 10

Editorial Directions, Inc.: E. Russell Primm and Emily J. Dolbear, Editors;
Flanagan Publishing Services, Photo Researcher

The Child's World®: Mary Berendes, Publishing Director

Printed in the United States of America.

Library of Congress Cataloging-in-Publication Data
Klingel, Cynthia Fitterer.
Football / by Cynthia Klingel and Robert B. Noyed.
p. cm. — (Wonder books)
"A level two reader."
Summary: Simple text describes the game of football, how it is played, and the equipment used.
Includes bibliographical references and index.
ISBN 1-56766-457-1 (lib. bdg. : alk. paper)
1. Football—Juvenile literature. [1. Football.] I. Noyed, Robert B. II. Title. III. Series: Wonder books (Chanhassen, MN.)
GV950.7 .K55 2003 2002015146